THIS WALKER BOOK BELONGS TO:

First published 1991 by Walker Books Ltd
87 Vauxhall Walk, London SE11 5HJ

This edition published 2008

4 6 8 10 9 7 5

This book has been typeset in New Century School Book

Printed in China

British Library Cataloguing in Publication Data:
a catalogue record for this book is available from the British Library

ISBN 978-1-4063-1331-4

www.walker.co.uk

My Grandpa is AMAZING

Nick Butterworth

WALKER BOOKS
AND SUBSIDIARIES
LONDON • BOSTON • SYDNEY • AUCKLAND

My grandpa is amazing.

He builds fantastic sand-castles …

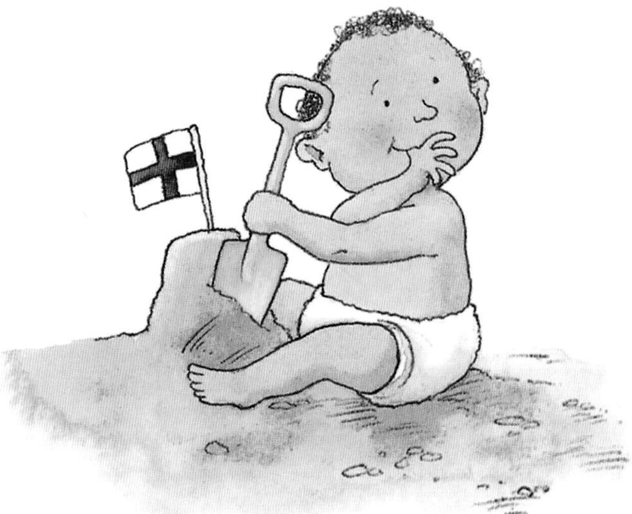

and he makes
marvellous drinks …

and he's
not at all afraid
of heights …

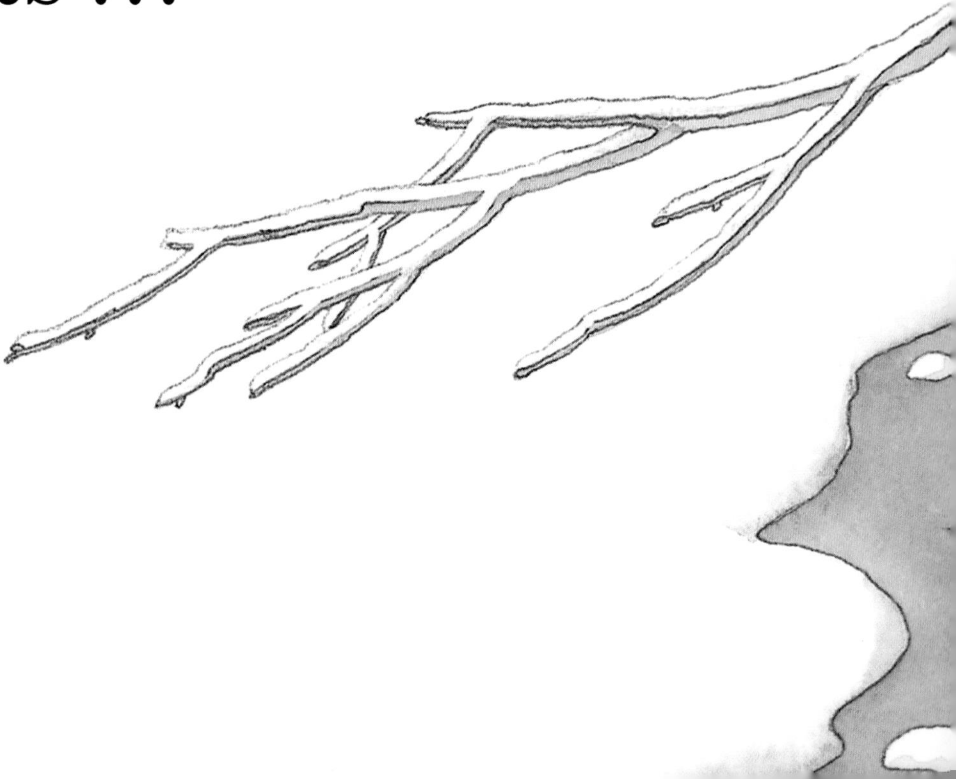

and he makes
wonderful flower
arrangements …

and he's a
brilliant driver …

10

and he knows
all about first aid …

and he's got an
amazing bike …

59

and he's a
terrific dancer …

and he's very, very,
very patient …

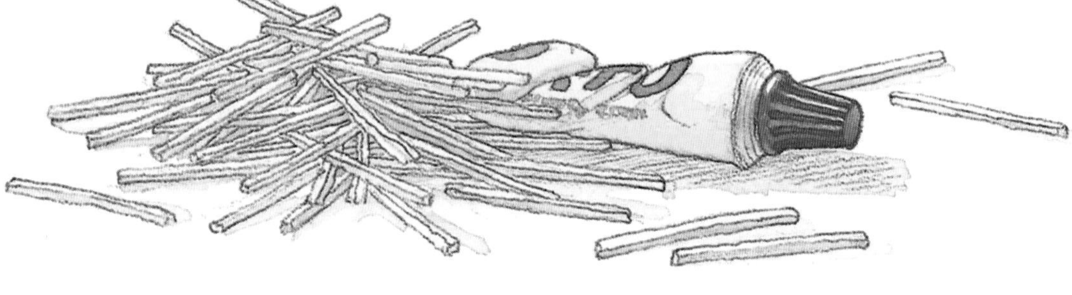

and he invents brilliant games.

It's great to have a grandpa like mine.

He's amazing!